Goldie
the Sunshine
Fairy

Dedicated to Liss Brothwell,
who is a little ray of sunshine

Special thanks to
Sue Mongredien

No part of this work may be reproduced, stored in a retrieval
system, or transmitted in any form or by any means, electronic,
mechanical, photocopying, recording, or otherwise, without written
permission of the publisher. For information regarding permission,
write to Rainbow Magic Limited, c/o HIT Entertainment,
830 South Greenville Avenue, Allen, TX 75002-3320.

ISBN-13: 978-0-439-81389-1
ISBN-10: 0-439-81389-1

20 19 18 17   13 14 15 16/0

Printed in the U.S.A.   40

Goldie
the Sunshine
Fairy

by Daisy Meadows

SCHOLASTIC INC.

New York   Toronto   London   Auckland   Sydney
Mexico City   New Delhi   Hong Kong   Buenos Aires

Jack Frost's
Ice Castle

Green Wood

Mrs. Fordham's House

The Park

Willow Hill

High St.

The Museum

Kirsty's House

Fields

Mudhole

N
W—E
S

Goblins green and goblins small,
I cast this spell to make you tall.
As high as the palace you shall grow.
My icy magic makes it so.

Then steal the rooster's magic feathers,
Used by the fairies to make all weathers.
Climate chaos I have planned
On Earth, and here, in Fairyland!

Contents

A Sunny Spell

"I feel like I'm going to melt," said Rachel Walker happily.

It was a hot summer afternoon and she and her friend, Kirsty Tate, were enjoying the sunshine in Kirsty's backyard. A bumblebee buzzed lazily around Mrs. Tate's sunflowers, and a single gust of wind blew through the yellow rosebushes.

The weather was so warm and sunny that Mr. and Mrs. Tate had given the  girls permission to camp out in the yard that night. Kirsty looked up from a jumble of tent poles and bright orange material. "It's been a perfect day," she agreed. "Let's hope tonight is perfect, too. It wouldn't be much fun to sleep out here in the rain!"

Rachel laughed, and then started untangling tent poles with her friend. "I think I'd rather take a shower in the *morning,* not in the middle of the night," she agreed.

Kirsty held up some poles. "Right. So how do we put this thing together?" she asked brightly.

Rachel scratched her head. "Well . . ." she began.

"Need some help?" came a voice from behind them.

"Dad!" said Kirsty, relieved. "Yes, please. We —" She turned to look at her father and burst out laughing.

Rachel spun around to see what was so funny. She had to bite her lip not to laugh, too. Mr. Tate was wearing the most enormous sunglasses she had ever seen!

Mr. Tate looked very pleased with himself. He wiggled the glasses up and down on his nose. "Do you like my new shades?" he asked.

"Well, yes," Kirsty said, trying to keep a straight face. "They're very . . . summery."

Mr. Tate knelt down and started putting the tent together. "The weather has been so strange all week, I didn't know whether to buy the sunglasses or not," he said. "I just hope it doesn't start snowing again!"

Rachel and Kirsty looked at each other but didn't say anything. The two friends shared a very special secret. They knew *exactly* why the weather had been so strange — Jack Frost had been messing it all up.

Doodle, the weather vane rooster, usually controlled the weather in Fairyland with his seven magic tail feathers and the help of the Weather Fairies. But mean Jack Frost had sent his goblins to steal Doodle's feathers. Without the feathers, the weather in Fairyland and the real world had gone completely crazy. Rachel and Kirsty were helping the Weather Fairies to get them back, but until then, Doodle was just a regular weather vane on top of the Tates' barn.

The day before, with the help of Pearl the Cloud Fairy, Kirsty and Rachel had returned the Cloud Feather to Doodle. But even though the girls had found the Snow Feather, the Breeze Feather, and the Cloud Feather, they still had four feathers left to find.

"There!" said Mr. Tate, stepping back and admiring the finished tent. "It's all yours."

"Thanks, Dad," Kirsty said as he walked away. She put two sleeping bags inside the tent and then flopped down on the grass. "Phew!" she said, and whistled. "It's still so hot! I hope it cools down soon, or we'll never be able to sleep in

there." Rachel was frowning and looking
at her watch.

"Kirsty," she said slowly. "Have
you noticed where the sun is?"

Kirsty looked up and
pointed. "Right there,
in the sky," she
replied.

"Yes, but look
how high it is,"
Rachel insisted.
"It hasn't even
started setting yet."

Kirsty glanced
at her watch. "But
it's seven-thirty,"
she said, frowning.
"That can't be
right."

Before Rachel could reply, there was a loud *pop!*

"What was that?" she whispered.

Pop! Pop! Pop!

"It sounds like it's coming from the other side of those bushes," Kirsty said, her eyes wide. "But there's only a cornfield over there."

Pop! Pop! Pop!

Cautiously, the girls peeked over the hedge to see what was making all the noise. And then they both gasped out loud.

Goldie Drops In

"I don't believe it," Kirsty said, rubbing her eyes. "Is that what I think it is?"

Pop! Pop! Pop!

Rachel nodded. "Popcorn!" she whispered.

It was an amazing sight. The sun was so hot that the corn in the field was cooking — and turning into popcorn!

Both girls stared as fluffy golden popcorn bounced everywhere. It looked like the field was one huge popcorn machine at the movie theater! The delicious smell of popcorn drifted over the bushes, and both girls sniffed hungrily.

Kirsty and Rachel looked at each other and grinned.

"There's definitely magic in the air," Kirsty said.

"It must be the goblin with the Sunshine Feather," Rachel agreed, feeling her heart beat faster.

Both girls looked hard at the field,

hoping to spot a goblin lurking
somewhere, but it was hard to
see clearly through the
popcorn. It was
tumbling and
twirling in
the air like
a sandstorm.
Rachel suddenly
grabbed Kirsty's hand.
"Look!" she cried.
Zooming above the
field was a twinkling yellow
light. It was zigzagging
through the air between the
popcorn, heading straight toward
them. As it came closer, the air
above the field seemed to glitter with a
thousand golden sparkles.

Both girls could see a pair of delicate
wings beating quickly, and the glimmer
of a tiny wand.

"It's Goldie the Sunshine Fairy,"
whispered Rachel, smiling.

The girls held their breath as the fairy
weaved in and out of the bouncing
popcorn, dodging each piece. Then she
swooped down and landed on the bushes

in front of them. "Phew!"
she said with a laugh.
"Talk about a bumpy
ride!"

Kirsty and Rachel
watched as Goldie
shook popcorn dust
from her glittering
wings. Her face was
framed by long, curly,
blond hair, and she wore a
dress of fiery reds, yellows, and oranges. A
tiny gold tiara sparkled in her hair, and
shiny red bracelets glimmered on her wrists.

"Hello again," said Goldie. "I've
heard all about how you've helped
Crystal, Abigail, and Pearl. You did a
wonderful job finding their weather
feathers!"

Rachel and Kirsty grinned at each other proudly.

"The goblin who has the Sunshine Feather can't be far away," Goldie continued, looking up at the sky. The sun still blazed as brightly as ever.

"That's what we thought, too," Kirsty said. "There's a farm on the other side of this field. Should we start looking there?"

"Good idea," Goldie replied cheerfully. Her face fell as soon as she turned back toward the cornfield. Popcorn was still whizzing through the air like hot white bumblebees. "But is there another way across the field?"

Goblin on the Loose!

"I don't like the idea of dodging that popcorn again." Goldie sighed. She leaned back to examine a little mark on one of her wings. "I almost burned myself last time."

"There's a path that runs down the side of the field to the farm," Kirsty told her. "I'll ask Mom if we can go for a quick walk before bedtime."

Minutes later, the three of them were on
their way. The air was shimmering with
heat. There were cracks in the ground
where the dirt had become hardened by
the sun, flowers wilted along the sides
of the path, and the grass had turned dry

and brown. There wasn't the slightest
breath of wind in the air. Once the girls
and Goldie reached the farm, they started
searching for the goblin.

First, they peeked into the stables. Two very hot horses were inside, hiding from the sun. "Hello," Goldie said. "You haven't seen a goblin hanging around here, have you?"

One of the horses shook her mane.

"All we've seen today is this stable," she said. "And there are no goblins in here."

"It's too hot to go outside," the other horse whinnied.

Next, the girls and
Goldie slipped
into the barn
where the cows
stayed. The
cows were all
half-asleep in the heat.
There was no goblin there, either!
At last, the three friends came
to the duck pond. They
wondered if the goblin
might be cooling off in
the water, but there was
no sign of him — or the
Sunshine Feather.

"You should ask the
pigs," one duck quacked
helpfully from a shady spot
in the cattails. "They've been grumbling

all day about something. Plus, pigs are nosy. They're always sniffing around! If there's a goblin on the farm, they'll know about it."

Goldie politely thanked the duck.

"I think I hear the pigs over this way," Rachel said, walking around the side of the farmhouse. Soon they could all hear the pigs grunting and squealing. The duck was right! The pigs seemed very upset about something. But they all turned to look curiously at Goldie when she flew over to them.

Goldie fluttered down and
landed on the biggest
pig's snout. "What's
wrong?" she asked
kindly.

The pig squinted at
the golden fairy in front
of his little blue eyes. "It's
like this," he began in a
squeaky voice. "It's been so hot that
the farmer added some cold water
to the mudhole, so that us pigs could
keep nice and cool." He twitched his
ears indignantly. "But someone else has
stolen our spot in the mud — and he
won't let us in!"

"It's not fair," a piglet squealed,
running up to Rachel and Kirsty. "We're
so hot! It's not fair!"

"No, it's not," Kirsty agreed, giving him a pat on the head.

"That sounds like the kind of trick a goblin would play!" Rachel pointed out. "Where is the mudhole?"

The pigs gave them directions, and the girls set off for the mudhole with Goldie flying above them. It seemed to get hotter and hotter as they walked. Rachel crossed her fingers. She was sure that they would find a goblin in the mud.

Who else would be mean enough to stop the pigs from cooling off in their own mud pool?

The girls hadn't been walking for very long when they heard someone singing in a croaky voice:

"I've been having so much fun
Blasting out this golden sun.
It's roasting, toasting, popcorn weather.
Oh, how I love my Sunshine Feather!"

Kirsty, Rachel, and Goldie all ducked behind a nearby tree and carefully peeked out. There, covered in thick, wet mud, was an extremely cheerful goblin. He waved the Sunshine Feather in the air while he sang. Each time the feather moved, golden sunbeams flooded from its tip, making the air feel even hotter.

Every time he got to the end of his
song, the goblin started all over again,
splashing his feet in the mud as he sang.
"I've been having so much fun . . ."

"What should we do?" Kirsty
whispered. The
goblin held on
to the feather
so tightly, it
looked like
it would be
impossible to take
it away from him.

Goldie twirled
around in frustration.

"I hate seeing him with my Sunshine
Feather," she muttered, folding her arms
across her chest. "Look, he got mud all
over it!"

Rachel frowned. "Maybe we could
distract him somehow, then run over and
grab the feather while he's looking the
other way."

"I don't
know about
running
through all
that slippery
mud," Kirsty
said quietly,
eyeing the
mudhole
doubtfully.
"We'll probably
fall over. And look,
the goblin is right in the middle of it.
He'll be able to see us coming way
before we get there."

They moved farther away from the mudhole so that they could figure out what to do next without the goblin overhearing. But after a few minutes, Rachel held up her hand. "Shh! What's that noise?" she whispered in alarm.

A Confused Goblin

Kirsty, Rachel, and Goldie held their breath and listened to the strange new sound. It was a loud, wheezing, rumbling noise, somewhere between a grunt and a hiss.

Grumble-sshhh, grumble-sshhh, grumble-sshhh . . .

The sound was coming from the direction

of the mudhole. Kirsty and Rachel crept
back to the tree and peeked out from
behind it, wondering what sort of
terrifying creature had appeared.

When Rachel saw what was making
the noise, though, she had to clap her
hand over her mouth to stop herself from
laughing out loud. The wheezy rumble
was coming from the goblin — he was
snoring!

"At least he isn't singing anymore,"
Kirsty whispered, laughing.

Goldie fluttered her wings
hopefully when she saw
that the goblin was
asleep, and she flew
a little closer to the
Sunshine Feather. But
her face fell when she
saw just how tightly the
goblin was clutching
the feather to his chest.
Goldie flew back to the girls,
shaking her head. "If I try to pull it out
of his hand, the goblin is sure to wake
up," she told them. "How are we going
to get that feather?"

Kirsty smiled. "Maybe we could . . ."
she began thoughtfully. Then she grinned
from ear to ear. "Yes! That could work!"
she said.

Without another word, Kirsty began running back toward her house. "I'll be back in a minute," she called over her shoulder.

Rachel and Goldie watched her go. They were both dying to know what Kirsty was up to. Luckily, they didn't have to wait very long. When Kirsty came back, she looked quite different!

"What is she wearing?"
Goldie whispered to
Rachel as Kirsty ran
toward them.

"Her dad's
sunglasses,"
Rachel replied,
staring at her
friend in
disbelief. She
was starting to
wonder if
Kirsty had been
in the sun for too
long. Why had she
brought the enormous
sunglasses back with her?
And why was she carrying a
fishing pole?

Kirsty grinned at the confused expressions on her friends' faces. "I'll explain everything," she promised, propping the fishing pole and sunglasses up in the tree branches. "But first, Rachel and I need to shrink to fairy size." Both Kirsty and Rachel had been given beautiful gold lockets by the Fairy Queen. Inside each locket was magical fairy dust. A tiny pinch of the sparkling dust turned the girls into fairies in the blink of an eye!

Kirsty and Rachel both pulled out their lockets and sprinkled themselves with fairy dust. It glittered a bright sunshine-yellow in the light and then — *whoosh* — they shrank smaller and smaller and smaller. The tree next to them looked enormous as the girls shrank to Goldie's size.

Kirsty and Rachel fluttered their wings happily. They both loved being fairies!

"Now," Kirsty said. "Let's fly up into the tree and I'll tell you my plan."

The three friends all perched near the fishing pole, and Goldie and Rachel watched as Kirsty carefully balanced the sunglasses on the end of the fishhook.

"We're going to let the fishing line out very slowly," Kirsty said, "and lower the sunglasses right down onto the goblin's nose."

"Why?" Rachel asked, confused.

"I don't know if they'll look good on him," Goldie said.

Kirsty shook her head, trying not to laugh.

"With sunglasses on, everything will look dark to him," she whispered. "With a bit of luck, the goblin will think the Sunshine Feather is broken!"

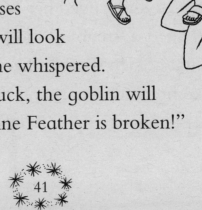

Goldie clapped her hands in delight. "Oh, what a great idea!" she cried. "I love to play tricks on those mean old goblins."

Very carefully, Kirsty, Rachel, and Goldie turned the handle of the fishing rod and lowered the sunglasses all the way down in front of the goblin. Kirsty held her breath as the sunglasses landed right on his big nose. Perfect! The girls reeled in the fishing line, and Goldie waved her wand in the air. It released a stream of magical fairy dust. Little golden sparkles fizzed and popped like firecrackers around the goblin's head until he woke up with a start.

He opened his eyes and blinked when
he saw that everything around him had
gotten dark. "My feather's broken!" he
moaned, giving it a shake. "Shine, sun!"
he commanded.

Of course, the girls knew that the
Sunshine Feather wasn't broken. As soon
as the goblin shook it, the sun became
brighter than ever. But as far as the goblin
could see, the world was still dark.

He waved the feather again. "I said, shine!" he ordered. The sun shone like it was the middle of the day, but Goldie and her friends realized that the goblin thought it looked like night. He shook the feather two more times and the sun shone

hotter and brighter, but the goblin saw only darkness. As far as he could tell, the Sunshine Feather was not working. "Broken!" he announced angrily, and he threw the feather away in disgust.

Just then, Goldie darted out of the tree
like a little golden firework.
While the goblin was still
muttering to himself, Goldie
swooped down and grabbed
the feather from the mud.

"Thank you!" she
called, hugging the
feather tightly as
she flew back to
the girls. Kirsty's
plan had worked!

With another
sprinkle of fairy dust,
Rachel and Kirsty turned
themselves human again.
They grabbed the fishing
rod and started scrambling
down from the tree.

But the goblin spotted the girls and jumped to his feet. As he did, the sunglasses bounced on his nose.

"Sunglasses?" he exclaimed, reaching up to grab the glasses in confusion. He pushed them onto the top of his head and squinted at the girls in the dazzling sunlight. "You tricked me!" he yelled when he saw Goldie clutching the Sunshine Feather. "Come back with that feather!"

Kirsty and Rachel looked at each other in fear. Now that Jack Frost's goblins were so big, they seemed scarier than ever. And this one looked *very* angry at having been tricked.

He shook his fist and headed straight toward the girls.

"*Run!*" shouted Kirsty.

Happy Pigs

Rachel grabbed Kirsty's hand and they both sprinted toward the farmhouse as fast as their feet would carry them. The goblin wasn't far behind, making a horrible growling sound in his throat as he ran.

"Give me back that feather! Give it back!" he yelled angrily.

Rachel's heart thumped in her chest. The goblin was closing in on them. She could hear his breathing. The goblin stretched out his hand to grab her and Rachel gasped.

"Got y —" the goblin began. Then his voice turned from anger to confusion. "Hey! What's going on?"

In a swirl of dancing sunbeams, Goldie
had waved the Sunshine Feather and
pointed it straight at the goblin. Now
the sun beat down fiercely upon him —
and the thick mud that covered
him started to dry rapidly. As his legs
became stiff and heavy with the
hardening mud, the goblin slowed down.
Then the mud dried completely, and the
goblin couldn't move at all.

"No-o-o!" he wailed.

Despite having been so scared just a few seconds before, the girls found themselves smiling at the goblin now. "It's a goblin statue!" Rachel exclaimed, laughing.

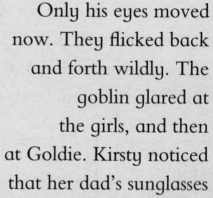

Only his eyes moved now. They flicked back and forth wildly. The goblin glared at the girls, and then at Goldie. Kirsty noticed that her dad's sunglasses were still perched on top of the goblin's head. She took a cautious step toward him, then another. The goblin didn't move, so Kirsty marched right up to him and carefully grabbed the glasses.

"I'll take these back now, I think," she
said. "If I'd known that these sunglasses
would be so useful, I'd never have
laughed at Dad for wearing them!" she
told Rachel.

Goldie and the girls made their way
back to the farmhouse. The pigs were
waiting expectantly for them.

"The mudhole is all yours again,"
Goldie told the pigs in her sweet voice.
"You'll see a new goblin statue nearby,"
she added. "But don't worry. I don't
think he'll be in any hurry to go back
into the mud."

The pigs grunted happily and trotted off toward their cool mud pool. The smallest piglet nuzzled Kirsty and Rachel's legs before he went. "Thank you!" he squealed.

Rachel watched the pigs go. "What will happen to the goblin?" she asked. "He won't have to stay there forever, will he?"

Goldie's eyes twinkled mischievously. "Not forever, no," she said. "The dried mud will wash off as soon as it rains." She smiled cheerfully. "But Jack Frost won't be happy with him when he finds out we got the Sunshine Feather back!"

Twilight Magic

Now that the three friends were out of danger, Goldie expertly waved the Sunshine Feather. The sun began to set, just like it was supposed to. The girls watched as the sky turned orange, pink, and a deep red.

"Let's bring the Sunshine Feather back

to Doodle," Kirsty said. "And then we'd better go to bed!"

Rachel was yawning. "It's been another busy day, hasn't it?" She smiled.

As the sun set, the warmth quickly faded away. The girls soon found themselves shivering in their thin shirts. Goldie fluttered above them with the Sunshine Feather, waving it gently. A few sunbeams flooded onto Rachel and Kirsty's bare arms to keep them warm.

It was almost dark by the time they all
got back to Kirsty's garden. They could
just barely see the silhouette of Doodle
on top of the barn roof.

Goldie flew up to give
the rooster back his
magic feather. As she
did, Doodle came to
life. His fiery feathers
glowed brilliantly in
the twilight. He
turned to look at
Rachel and Kirsty.
"Will come —" he
squawked urgently.
But before he could say
any more, the magic drained
away. Doodle's colors faded and he
became a rusty old weather vane again.

Every time the girls returned one of
Doodle's feathers, the rooster came to
life for a few seconds and squawked
a word or two. Rachel frowned as
she pieced together all the words that
Doodle had said so far. "Beware!
Jack Frost will come . . ." she
murmured. An icy shiver shot down
her spine, as if Jack Frost was already
there. "I think it's a warning, Kirsty.
Let's hope he doesn't come soon!"

Goldie looked worried. "Take
care of yourselves. And thank you for
everything," she said. She blew them a
stream of fairy kisses that sparkled in
the darkening sky. "I must go back
to Fairyland now. Good-bye!"

Kirsty and Rachel watched Goldie fly

away. Soon she was nothing more than a tiny golden speck in the distance. Then, just as the girls were about to get ready for bed, they heard footsteps. Mr. Tate came out of the house, looking around with a puzzled expression on his face. "Did I just hear a rooster crowing?" he asked.

"A rooster? At this time of day?" Kirsty replied innocently.

Mr. Tate frowned. "I must be hearing things," he said, turning to go back inside. "Good night, girls. Sleep well." He glanced up at Doodle as he headed back toward the house. "I'm sure that weather vane had a smaller tail before," he muttered, then shook his head. "Now I'm seeing things, too! It's definitely time to call it a night. . . ."

Kirsty and Rachel smiled at each other. "He's right!" Kirsty said. "Doodle *does* have four feathers now. We only have three more feathers to find. I wonder which one will be next!"

THE WEATHER FAIRIES

Rachel and Kirsty have helped Crystal,
Abigail, Pearl, and Goldie find their
feathers. Now it's time to help

Evie the
Mist Fairy!

A Misty Morning

"Wake up, sleepyhead!" cried Kirsty
Tate, as she jumped out of bed and
started to get dressed.

Her friend, Rachel Walker, was asleep
in the extra bed in Kirsty's room. She was
staying with Kirsty and her parents in
Wetherbury. Sleepily, she rolled over and
opened her eyes. "I was dreaming that we
were back in Fairyland," she told Kirsty.
"The weather was mixed up — sunny

and snowing all at the same time — and
Doodle was trying to fix it." Doodle, the
magic weather rooster, had been on
Rachel's mind a lot lately, because she
and Kirsty were on an important mission
with the Weather Fairies!

Every day in Fairyland, Doodle and
the Weather Fairies used his magic tail
feathers to make the weather. Each of
the seven feathers controlled a different
kind of weather, and each of the seven
Weather Fairies worked with one
feather. The system was perfect until
mean Jack Frost sent his goblins to steal
Doodle's magic feathers.

The goblins took the feathers into the
human world, and when poor Doodle
followed them out of Fairyland, he
was transformed into a rusty metal

weather vane. Since Rachel and Kirsty
had found the Rainbow Fairies together,
the Queen of the Fairies had asked them
to help find and return Doodle's magic
feathers.

In the meantime, Fairyland's weather
was all mixed up — and the goblins had
been using the feathers to cause trouble
in the human world too.

"Poor Doodle," Kirsty said, looking out
of the window at the weather vane on
top of the old barn. Her dad had found
Doodle lying in the park, and brought
him home for their barn roof.

"Hopefully we'll find another magic
feather today," Kirsty continued. "We
already have four of the stolen feathers.
We just need to find the other three and
then Doodle will get his magic back."

"Yes," Rachel agreed, brightening at the thought. "But I have to go home in three days, so we don't have very long!" As she gazed out at the blue sky, a wisp of silvery mist caught her eye. "Look — that cloud is shaped just like a feather!" she said.

Kirsty looked up, too. "I can't see anything."

Rachel looked again, but the wispy shape had disappeared. "Maybe I imagined it," she sighed. The memory of the dream fizzed in her tummy like lemonade bubbles. It felt like a magical start to the day.

RAINBOW magic

THE JEWEL FAIRIES

They Make Fairyland Sparkle!

SCHOLASTIC
www.scholastic.com
www.rainbowmagiconline.com

HiT entertainment

JEWEL

RAINBOW magic™

There's Magic in Every Series!

The Rainbow Fairies
The Weather Fairies
The Jewel Fairies
The Pet Fairies
The Fun Day Fairies
The Petal Fairies
The Dance Fairies
The Music Fairies
The Sports Fairies
The Party Fairies
The Ocean Fairies
The Night Fairies
The Magical Animal Fairies
The Princess Fairies
The Superstar Fairies

Read them all!

■ SCHOLASTIC

scholastic.com
rainbowmagiconline.com

HIT entertainment

RMFAIRY7

SPECIAL EDITION

Three Books in Each One—
More Rainbow Magic Fun!

Joy the Summer Vacation Fairy
Holly the Christmas Fairy
Kylie the Carnival Fairy
Stella the Star Fairy
Shannon the Ocean Fairy
Trixie the Halloween Fairy
Gabriella the Snow Kingdom Fairy
Juliet the Valentine Fairy
Mia the Bridesmaid Fairy
Flora the Dress-Up Fairy
Paige the Christmas Play Fairy
Emma the Easter Fairy
Cara the Camp Fairy
Destiny the Rock Star Fairy
Belle the Birthday Fairy
Olympia the Games Fairy
Selena the Sleepover Fairy
Cheryl the Christmas Tree Fairy
Florence the Friendship Fairy
Lindsay the Luck Fairy

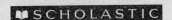

SCHOLASTIC

scholastic.com
rainbowmagiconline.com

HIT entertainment

RMSPECIAL10

RAINBOW magic

These activities are magical!

■ SCHOLASTIC

www.scholastic.com
www.rainbowmagiconline.com

HIT entertainment

RMACTIV